to us a child is born...

Wonderful Counselor,

Mighty God,

Everlasting Father,

Prince of Peace.

Isaiah 9:6

For my parents

who introduced me to the **Christ Child**

and taught me about that first Bethlehem night

in the arms of a loving family

Published by Concordia Publishing House
3558 S. Jefferson Avenue, St. Louis, MO 63118-3968
1-800-325-3040 • www.cph.org

Text copyright © 2005 by Julie Stiegemeyer
Illustrations copyright © 2005 Concordia Publishing House

Manufactured in China

1 2 3 4 5 6 7 8 9 10   14 13 12 11 10 09 08 07 06 05

Bethlehem Night

Written by Julie Stiegemeyer

Illustrated by Gina Capaldi

CONCORDIA PUBLISHING HOUSE · SAINT LOUIS

On a Bethlehem night
so starry and bright,

down a long dusty road
with a delicate load,

an old donkey sways,
and a young woman prays.

Mary's tired and sore;
every step is a chore.

Husband Joseph is strong
as God helps them along.

And they **trust in God's Word,**
know their prayers will be heard

on that Bethlehem night
so starry and bright.

They are scared and alone
as the chilly winds moan.

Mary's baby is near,
but why do they fear?

For this night was foretold
in the Scriptures of old,

that this baby God gave,
from our sins, He will save.

From a loud, crowded inn,
they are searching again.

On a bustling street
filled with hurrying feet,

no one welcomes a guest;
there is no place to rest

on that Bethlehem night
so starry and bright.

Oh, where will they stay
since there's no room today?

Soon this child will be born,
but they wander forlorn.

At last, in a dark space,
Joseph finds them a place.

In a damp stable cold
God's love will enfold—

just a shelter to sleep,
home for oxen and sheep—

gentle creatures will be
first the Savior to see

on that Bethlehem night
so starry and bright.

Then the animals hush,
and the howling winds shush.

At last breathing a sigh,
mother hears baby's cry,

and **God comes to the earth**
through this heavenly birth

on that Bethlehem night
so starry and bright.

In a pasture nearby,
  shepherds' lambs bleat and sigh,

    all is drowsy and still
      in that field, until...

        with a burst through the night,
          angels shine heaven's light.

"Gentle shepherds, don't fear!
For your Savior is here!

"In a manger He lies
    under Bethlehem skies—

    just a new baby small
        in an old cattle stall."

The shepherds then ran,
so amazed at God's plan.

Falling on bended knee,
their dear Savior they see:

Jesus, cradled in hay,
in a manger He lay.

And the shepherds adore;
they are frightened no more.

Then with swift-running feet
through the alleys and streets,

the shepherds then tell
how **God came here to dwell,**

came among us to live,
came, a man, to forgive.

And their good news is ours,
from that night full of stars,

and on Christmas each year,
Jesus' story we hear:

How this tiny babe's birth
brought **salvation to earth**

on that Bethlehem night
so starry and bright.